When the wicked queen banishes Snow White from the castle, the beautiful princess is left alone in the forest. But the seven dwarfs help her and all is well until, one day, the queen comes to the forest to look for her.

British Library Cataloguing in Publication Data
Disney, Walt
    Walt Disney's Snow White and the seven dwarfs.—
    (Ladybird Disney series. no. 845; 5)
    I. Title   II. Grimm, Jacob. Schneewittchen
    813'.54[J]   PZ7
    ISBN 0-7214-0876-1

Snow White
and the Seven Dwarfs

Ladybird Books

Once upon a time, long ago, there
lived a princess called Snow White.
She lived with her father, the king,
and her stepmother, the queen, in a
tall castle which stood at the edge
of a deep green forest.

Snow White was very beautiful.
Her skin was as white as snow, her
hair as black as ebony wood, and
her lips were as red as a rose.

The queen was also very beautiful but she was proud. She knew that *she* was the most beautiful lady in the land.

The queen had a magic mirror and every day she would look into it and whisper:
Magic mirror on the wall,
Who is the fairest one of all?

And the mirror would always reply:
You, O Queen, are the fairest of
*   them all.*

The queen would smile because she knew that the mirror always spoke the truth.

One day the queen came as usual to look into the magic mirror. She whispered the special words and waited for the mirror to answer:

Famed is thy beauty, Majesty,
But behold – a lovely maid I see.
Alas, she is more fair than thee,
Lips as red as rose, hair as black as ebony,
Skin as white as snow.

The queen stamped her foot. "Snow White is *more* beautiful!" she screamed. "It cannot be!" And then she stormed out of the room.

From that day, the wicked queen hated poor Snow White. Every day she grew more and more jealous of Snow White's beauty.

The queen took away Snow White's fine clothes and dressed her in rags instead. She made the princess do all the cleaning and

polishing in the castle, every day.
And every night, Snow White
would dream of a handsome prince
who would come one day and carry
her off to his castle.

One morning the queen sent for the huntsman. "Take Snow White out into the forest," she ordered. "I never want to see her again."

Next morning, the huntsman and Snow White set off into the forest.

The huntsman knew that the queen wanted him to kill Snow White but he loved the little princess and could not do such a thing.

"Run away into the forest," he said. "The queen will think that I have killed you so you must never come back to the castle again."

The huntsman left poor Snow White alone. The trees were full of dark shadows and strange noises. She ran as far as she could until she came to a cottage, hidden deep in the forest.

Snow White knocked at the door
and when no one answered, she
went inside. She wondered who
could live in such a tiny house.
She looked around the room –
everything was so small!

There were seven dusty little chairs
at the table. In the sink, there were
seven dirty spoons and bowls. And
in the bedroom, there were seven
little beds.

"Perhaps some children live here,"
Snow White thought. "But how
dirty everything is!" Quickly, she
dusted the house and made
everything look neat and tidy.
Then she was tired so she lay down
to rest and fell fast asleep.

When night-time came, the masters
of the house returned from work.
They were seven dwarfs who
worked in the diamond mines, deep
in the heart of the mountain.

They knew at once that something had changed. Their house was clean! The bowls and spoons had been put away and the floor had been swept. "What's happened?" they asked each other.

"Maybe it's ghosts or goblins,"
said one of the dwarfs, in a
trembling voice.

"Careful, men! Search every nook
and cranny," said another, sternly.

Then the dwarfs crept into the
bedroom.

"Oh!" they gasped, when they saw the beautiful princess. "Who are you and what are you doing in our house?"

"My name is Snow White," said the princess. "I am hiding from the wicked queen who wants to kill me! Who are you?"

"I'm Grumpy."

"I'm Doc."

"I'm Bashful."

"I'm Sleepy."

22

"I'm Sneezy."

"I'm Happy."

"And he's Dopey," they
all shouted together.

"I'm very pleased to meet you all," said Snow White, politely. "If you let me stay here, I'll work hard and keep house for you." The dwarfs said that she could stay.

"Supper is not quite ready," said Snow White, smiling. "You'll just have time to wash."

"I knew there was a catch to it," said Grumpy. "Well, I'd like to see anybody make *me* wash!"

"All right!" said Doc. And they tossed Grumpy into the wash-tub and scrubbed him clean. Then they all sat down to a delicious supper.

The princess kept her promise.
Every day she cleaned the cottage,
made the beds, and baked pies
and cakes.

The dwarfs had never known
anyone who was so good and kind.
They all loved Snow White and she
was so happy that she soon forgot
all about the wicked queen.

Now the queen had been very pleased when the huntsman had told her that Snow White was dead. But when she next whispered the special words into the magic mirror, the mirror replied:

Snow White, who dwells with the seven little men,
Is as fair as you and as fair again.

When she heard this, the queen went pale, for she knew that Snow White must still be alive. "The huntsman has tricked me!" she screamed. "This time, I will think of something that will make an end of her once and for all."

One day, after the seven dwarfs
had gone to the diamond mines,
there came a tap-tapping at the
cottage door. Snow White opened
it and saw an old beggar-woman
standing on the step.

The woman was holding a basket,
full of apples. "Try my apples,
pretty maid," she said, smiling.
"They are magic wishing apples:
one bite and your dreams will come
true."

Snow White thought of the handsome prince in her dreams and took one of the apples. She bit into it and fell to the floor.

The old beggar-woman laughed.
"Nothing but a kiss from your
true-love can save you now,
Snow White."

Just then, the seven dwarfs
returned home from work. As they
came through the forest, they saw
a shadowy figure near the cottage.
"Look!" cried Doc. "It's the
wicked queen! After her, men!"
And they chased her through the
forest, towards the mountain.

The queen ran on but she slipped
on a ledge and fell down the side
of the mountain into a deep hole
between the rocks. She was never
seen again.

When the dwarfs came back to the cottage, they found Snow White lying on the floor. They tried everything to wake her but it was no good.

So they built a beautiful bed for
Snow White, made of crystal glass
and gold. They took her to a
special place in the forest and kept
watch, day and night.

Months passed. Snow White's bed
was covered with leaves, then
snow, and then the blossoms of
spring. Always, the princess looked
the same, just as if she were
sleeping.

A handsome prince from a nearby kingdom heard of the lovely princess sleeping in the forest. He rode there to see her. "How beautiful she is!" he said, kneeling down to kiss her.

The princess opened her eyes! She sat up on her golden bed and smiled. "She's awake! She's awake!" shouted the dwarfs. "The prince has broken the wicked queen's spell."

Snow White knew that this was the prince of her dreams. "Will you marry me and come to live in my father's palace?" he said. Snow White smiled and said that she would.

Then she said goodbye to the
dwarfs, who had been so kind to
her. "Don't be sad," she said.
"You can come to the palace
whenever you like and I promise to
visit you here in the forest, every
spring."

And so Snow White married the
prince and they lived happily
ever after.